The Adventures of MARY-KATE & ASHLEY™

THE CASE OF THE
· HOTEL ·
WHO·DONE·IT™

A novelization by Laura O'Neil

WILL SOLVE ANY CRIME · BY DINNER TIME™

DUALSTAR PUBLICATIONS PARACHUTE PRESS, INC.

SCHOLASTIC INC.

New York   Toronto   London   Auckland   Sydney

DUALSTAR PUBLICATIONS ™ PARACHUTE PRESS, INC.

Dualstar Publications
c/o Thorne and Company
1801 Century Park East
Los Angeles, CA 90067

Parachute Press, Inc.
156 Fifth Avenue
Suite 325
New York, NY 10010

Published by Scholastic Inc.

With special thanks to Robert Thorne, Harold Weitzberg,
and Hilton Hawaiian Village.

Printed in the U.S.A.
June 1997
ISBN: 0-590-88013-6
A B C D E F G H I J

Ready for Adventure?

It was the best of times. It was the worst of times. Actually it was bedtime when our great-grandmother would read us stories of mystery and suspense. It was then that we decided to be detectives.

The story you are about to read is one of the cases from the files of the Olsen and Olsen Mystery Agency. We call it *The Case Of The Hotel Who-Done-It*.

Our family was on vacation in a fabulous, fancy Hawaiian hotel. Ashley and I couldn't wait to splash in the pool, watch movies on the huge TV in our room, and order yummy food from room service—day and night! But first we had to catch a thief. Someone was robbing the hotel guests. But who was it? We didn't have a clue!

Ashley and I had solved hard cases before—but this case was no vacation. Could it be that Olsen and Olsen were through? No way! We had to find a way to crack this case. Because, no matter what, we always live up to our motto: Will Solve Any Crime By Dinner Time!

Chapter 1

"Aloha, bedroom!" I sang out. "Aloha, schoolbooks. Aloha, winter weather!"

Aloha is how you say good-bye in Hawaiian. It also means hello. But I was definitely saying good-bye, because my family was going on a winter vacation—to sunny Hawaii! I could hardly wait.

I grabbed my favorite pair of shorts and tossed them into my suitcase.

"Don't forget to say aloha to the Olsen and Olsen Mystery Agency," added my twin sister, Ashley. Ashley folded her flowered sundress and placed it neatly into her suitcase.

My name is Mary-Kate Olsen. Ashley and I are the Trenchcoat Twins. We solve crimes.

We love mysteries. We're detectives!

Ashley and I are both nine years old. We both have strawberry blond hair and big blue eyes.

We look alike. But we sure don't act alike.

Ashley likes to take her time doing everything. I like to jump right in!

And we don't always think alike, either.

"I think we'd better pack our laptop computers," I told Ashley.

"I don't think we should," Ashley said. "You know the rule—Mom and Dad said absolutely no detective work on this vacation!"

I groaned. "It's just not fair," I said. "Solving mysteries isn't work. It's fun!"

"Don't worry about it," Ashley told me. "We'll find plenty of mysteries to solve as soon as we come home again."

Mom stuck her head into our room. "Ready to go to the airport, girls?" she asked.

"Almost," Ashley replied.

"Well, hurry, please," Mom said. "We don't

want to miss our plane."

"Okay, Mom," Ashley said.

"Uh, Mom," I added. "I know we're not supposed to do detective work on vacation. But is it all right if Ashley and I bring along some books to read?"

"Of course," Mom told me. "Vacation is a great time for reading books. Now, finish your packing." She left our room and hurried downstairs.

I picked up two books from my bed. "Pack this, Ashley," I said. I handed her one of the books.

"This is my detective manual!" Ashley said in surprise.

Our great-grandmother Olive gave us our detective manuals. She loves mysteries as much as we do. She's the one who taught us how to be detectives.

"Mom said that reading is perfect for vacation," I told Ashley. "We might not be able to *solve* mysteries on this vacation—but we can still *read* about them."

"Great idea!" Ashley grinned.

"And you know, Mom never said we couldn't bring our detective equipment along," I added. "She just said we couldn't *use* it."

"Are you thinking what I'm thinking?" Ashley asked.

"I'm thinking that we'd better get up to the attic—and fast!"

Our detective agency is in the attic of our house. It's filled with detective equipment— our tape recorder, some fake noses and other disguises, our magnifying glasses, binoculars, walkie-talkies, and our laptop computers.

Ashley and I ran out the bedroom door and up to the attic. We quickly packed our equipment.

I was sliding my computer into my backpack, when I heard a strange, rumbling noise.

"What's that funny sound?" I asked.

"I don't know. But it's coming from over there," Ashley replied. She pointed at the desk that we shared.

We hurried to our desk. Our pet basset hound, Clue, lay curled up on the desk chair.

Clue is brown and white. She has floppy ears and a big, wet nose—perfect for sniffing out clues.

We call her our silent partner. She helps us solve mysteries.

Clue's eyes were closed, and she was sound asleep.

"Mystery solved," I said. "That funny noise is the sound of Clue—snoring!" Ashley and I giggled.

"Well, I have another mystery for you," Ashley said. She gazed down at Clue. "Why is Clue sleeping so much lately?"

"That's easy," I told her. "Clue is tired from her classes at obedience school."

Dad was sending Clue to Little Barker's

Obedience School. An obedience school is a place where dogs learn how to do tricks and follow orders.

Dad's friend sent his poodle, Stinger, to obedience school. Stinger learned all sorts of fancy tricks there. So Dad thought Clue should go, too.

"Too bad Clue will miss her last week of school," Ashley said.

"I know. I just hope she does okay on her obedience test," I added. "She has to take it right after we come home from vacation."

"She'll do fine," Ashley told me. "Clue is naturally obedient. I bet she'll get an A on that test."

"*Woof!*"

Clue woke up. She barked and sniffed my hand.

"It's a good thing you're awake, Clue," Ashley told her. "It's time to catch our plane."

Clue jumped to her feet. She gave a big yawn and stretched.

"Come on, Clue," I called.

Ashley and I headed down the stairs. "Let's see what kind of fun your super-duper snooper sniffs out—in Hawaii!"

Chapter 2

"This hotel room is awesome!" Ashley exclaimed.

Actually we had four rooms that were joined together. One room was like our living room at home. It was filled with couches, chairs, and a huge TV. The other three rooms were bedrooms—one for Mom and Dad, one for Trent and Lizzie, our brother and sister, and one for Ashley and me.

"Check this out!" I rushed over to a small refrigerator in the living room and flung open the door.

The refrigerator was packed with snacks. Candy, ice cream, and sodas filled every shelf.

"Incredible!" Ashley exclaimed, "And so is

this!" She showed me the menu for room service. "We can have hamburgers, chili dogs, and even a late-night pizza delivered right to our room!"

"And there's a TV with tons of movies to watch," I added.

"Who has time to watch dumb movies?" our big brother, Trent, asked. Trent is eleven, and sometimes he can be a real pain.

Trent threw open the curtains over a pair of sliding glass doors. The doors led onto a wide balcony. Beyond the balcony we could see the ocean. We watched the huge waves roll onto the beach below.

"Let me at those waves!" Trent exclaimed. "I'm going down to the beach to hang ten!"

"Hang ten what?" I asked.

"Hang ten toes over the end of a surfboard," Trent explained. "I'm going surfing!"

"But you don't know how to surf," I reminded him.

"I'll learn. I'll take surfing lessons." Trent

brushed his brown bangs off his forehead. "Can I, Dad?" he asked.

"Why not?" Dad said. "I might even try surfing myself." Dad turned to our little sister, Lizzie. "What do you want to do, Lizzie?" he asked.

"Whatever Mary-Kate and Ashley want to do," Lizzie answered.

Lizzie is six. She thinks we're great detectives. She always wants to follow us around.

"First, we're going to ride our bikes. Then we want to check out the video game room," I told Lizzie. "And you hate those games."

"Lizzie, you should come with me," Dad said. "We can swim in the hotel pool while Trent takes surfing lessons."

"Okay," Lizzie said. "I'd like that."

"Take Clue, too," Mom added. "She could use a walk."

Clue leaped up and ran to the balcony doors. She planted her paws on the doors and started barking.

"Down, girl," Mom told her. "Quiet!"

Clue ignored Mom and kept on barking. Mom and Dad both frowned.

"Clue will never pass her test at obedience school," Dad said. "She's not following orders at all!"

Dad pulled Clue away from the balcony. "Maybe she'll behave better outside," he said. Dad turned to Mom. "Don't you want to come with us?" he asked.

"Not now," Mom answered. She pulled the elastic from her ponytail and shook out her brown hair. "Right now I want to take a shower and freshen up," she said. "I'll meet you all later."

Dad left with Lizzie, Trent, and Clue.

Mom took off her new gold charm bracelet and placed it on a table near the balcony doors.

The bracelet was a present from Dad. It had a shiny gold charm of a palm tree hanging from it. Dad gave it to her so she would have something special to wear on our first Hawaiian vacation.

Mom opened the balcony doors to let in some fresh air. Then she hurried into the shower.

Ashley and I went down to the lobby. We rented two bikes. We rode our bikes all around the hotel grounds.

Everything was beautiful! We brought our bikes back to the hotel. Then we headed to the game room.

We played five different video games before we ran out of quarters.

We raced back to our room to ask Mom for more change. We found her standing by the balcony. She looked upset.

"What's wrong?" I asked.

"It's my charm bracelet," Mom said with a frown. "I left it on this table, but it's not here now."

"Maybe it fell or something. We'll help you look for it," I said.

Mom threw up her hands. "It has to be here somewhere," she said. "How could a bracelet just disappear?" She shook her head. "I'll check the bedroom, just in case," she added.

Mom disappeared into the other room. There was a loud knock on our door.

"Peter P. Plinkus here," a man's voice said. "I am the assistant to the assistant to the assistant manager. I'm here to welcome you to the hotel."

"Let Mr. Plinkus in," Mom called to us from the bedroom. "I'll be out in a minute."

We opened the door, and Mr. Plinkus stepped in. He wore a fancy gray suit with a gleaming white vest and a gray satin tie. He was tall and bald and had a big smile. But his smile faded when he saw the worried look on our faces.

"Is something wrong?" Mr. Plinkus asked.

"We can't find our mom's new bracelet," I told him. "It's missing."

Mr. Plinkus turned pale. "Oh, no!" he cried. "Not another one!" He wrung his hands.

"Not another what?" Ashley asked him.

"Not another robbery!" Mr. Plinkus exclaimed.

"A robbery?" Ashley and I exchanged looks of surprise.

"Do you mean things are being stolen from the guests in this hotel?" I asked.

"Yes, I'm sorry to say." Mr. Plinkus moaned. "How will I ever figure out who the thief is?" he asked. "It's a terrible mystery!"

"Mysteries are no problem for *us*," I said.

Mr. Plinkus looked more closely at Ashley and me. His eyes opened wide.

"Wait a minute!" he exclaimed. "You're the Trenchcoat Twins!"

"In person," Ashley said.

"Please," Mr. Plinkus said. "You must help me find the thief! No one will want to stay in this hotel if there are any more robberies.

I might even lose my job."

I pulled my detective notebook from my suitcase. "Don't worry," I said. "But first we need some information. Exactly how many robberies were there?"

"Three," Mr. Plinkus replied. "Monica Martin, the famous actress, was robbed first. Her silver necklace was stolen right from her room. Then Luigi Caprio was robbed. Luigi is a famous opera singer. His diamond belt buckle was stolen. And now your mother's bracelet is missing!"

Mr. Plinkus shook his head. "And all the robberies were right here on the fifth floor," he added.

I wrote down all the information.

"Are there any other guests on this floor?" Ashley asked.

"Just one," Mr. Plinkus replied. "Tex Tumbleweed. Mr. Tumbleweed is our most important guest."

Mr. Plinkus smiled proudly. "Tex is here

to make a movie about his life. He's looking for actors to star in it. The movie is called *The Singing Cowboy Gets Rich*."

"Sounds like a good story," Ashley said. "But I wonder why nothing was stolen from Mr. Tumbleweed."

"A-ha!" I said. "Maybe nothing was stolen from him because *he's* the one *doing* the stealing!"

Mr. Plinkus laughed. "I don't think Tex is the thief," he said. "He isn't a singing cowboy anymore. He's in the oil business now—and he's very, very rich. In fact, he's a billionaire! He doesn't need to steal anything."

Hmmmmm.

"I guess we need more information about this case," I said.

"Maybe we should talk to Tex," Ashley added. "And to Monica and Luigi, too. Could we meet them?"

"No problem," Mr. Plinkus replied. "Let's go down to the hotel lobby. I can point them out to you." Mr. Plinkus paused. "But I don't want the other guests to know about the robberies—or that you are detectives working on this case."

"Don't worry about that," I told him. I opened my backpack and pulled out a couple of fake noses and mustaches attached to two pairs of glasses.

"We'll wear these disguises. Then no one will know we're the Trenchcoat Twins," I explained.

"And I'll bring our other detective equipment," Ashley added.

Ashley grabbed her backpack. Inside were a pair of binoculars, a magnifying glass, and our walkie-talkies.

"Shall we go?" Mr. Plinkus asked, heading toward the door.

"Just a minute!" Mom's voice rang out as she stepped into the living room. "Where do you two think you're going?"

Uh-oh!

"I heard what Mr. Plinkus said," Mom told us. "But we had a rule about this vacation. Remember?"

"Sorry, Mom. We forgot!" I said. I turned to Mr. Plinkus. "We're not supposed to solve any mysteries on this vacation," I explained.

"I guess we can't help you after all," Ashley added.

Mr. Plinkus gulped. "But you *must* help me!" he begged. "You must catch the thief— and soon!"

"What do you say, Mom?" I asked. "Mr. Plinkus really needs our help."

"So do his guests. And you want your bracelet back—don't you, Mom?" Ashley added.

Mom looked at Mr. Plinkus, then at Ashley and me. She sighed.

"Well, all right," Mom said. "I guess this is an important case. But I don't want you to spend your whole vacation working."

"No problem," I said. "You know our

motto: will solve any crime—" I began.

"By dinner time," Ashley finished.

Yes! Olsen and Olsen were back on the job.

Chapter 4

We followed Mr. Plinkus into the elevator. Ashley pulled a walkie-talkie out of her backpack and handed it to him.

"Press the TALK button to talk and the LISTEN button to listen," she told him.

"You can use this to tell us when Monica, Luigi, or Tex comes into the lobby," I said.

"Or anyone who looks suspicious," Ashley added.

"Oh, how clever," Mr. Plinkus said.

The elevator stopped at the lobby, and we all got out. The lobby was huge. Ashley and I found the perfect place to hide. We ducked behind a tall plant in a big pot. We pulled on our disguises. I turned on our walkie-talkie. Ashley opened her detective notebook.

Mr. Plinkus hurried over to the front desk. We watched as the hotel guests stopped to get their mail and their messages.

"Heads up!" Mr. Plinkus whispered into his walkie-talkie.

I pressed the TALK button on mine. "What is it?" I whispered. Then I pressed the LISTEN button again.

"Someone interesting is coming," Mr. Plinkus replied.

I peeked from behind the potted plant and groaned. "That's nobody interesting," I told him. "That's our brother, Trent!"

Trent was heading across the lobby, holding a rented surfboard on top of his head. He was trying to look like a cool surfer dude. Dad and Lizzie hurried after him. Clue pulled Dad along on her leash.

Mr. Plinkus set his walkie-talkie down on the counter. He left the LISTEN button on. That way Ashley and I could hear everything that was being said.

"Look at that cute bird!" Lizzie shouted.

A beautiful white bird flew across the lobby. It was huge—almost two feet tall. It had a long tail, a bright yellow beak, and a few yellow feathers on the top of its head. It landed on a fancy metal perch at the front desk.

"This is Elvis, my pet cockatoo," Mr. Plinkus said.

"Oooh! Can I pet him?" Lizzie asked.

"Woof! Woof!"

Clue leaped up at Elvis. Elvis flapped his white wings. The yellow feathers at the top of his head stood straight up.

"Down, girl!" Dad told Clue.

"Down, girl!" Elvis squawked, imitating Dad's voice.

"Wow! He sounds just like you, Dad," Lizzie said in surprise.

Dad tugged Clue's leash and pulled her away from the desk. "Come on, Clue. You too, Trent and Lizzie," he said. "Let's get

Mom and bring her outside. It would be great to have a swim in the ocean."

They crossed the lobby to the elevator.

"Red alert! Red alert!" Mr. Plinkus called into his walkie-talkie. "Tex Tumbleweed approaching the front desk!"

I whipped out Ashley's binoculars for a closer look. I saw a tall man in a straw hat and jeans strolling in through the main door of the hotel. Around his neck he wore a thin string tie. The tie was held in place by a shiny, star-shaped silver clasp.

"Good afternoon, Mr. Tumbleweed. How are you today, sir?" Mr. Plinkus asked. "You look wonderful!"

"Howdy, Plinkus," Tex said with a heavy Texas accent. "I *feel* wonderful!"

Tex fed Elvis some sunflower seeds. "That's a mighty cute chicken," he told Mr. Plinkus.

Ashley and I giggled. "He's not a chicken," Ashley said.

Tex crumpled the empty sunflower seed bag and tossed it into a wastebasket.

"I'm out of sunflower seeds again." Tex sighed. "I just love those little seeds."

"Love those seeds!" Elvis repeated.

"Elvis really *does* love them," Mr. Plinkus said.

Ashley flipped open her detective notebook and scribbled some notes. INFORMATION: Tex loves sunflower seeds. So does Elvis, the cockatoo.

"Why are you writing that?" I asked her.

"Remember what Great-grandma Olive always says," Ashley told me. "Pay attention to details and keep an open mind. You never know which facts are going to be important."

Our walkie-talkie squawked. "I'm going up to my room now," we heard Tex tell Mr. Plinkus. "I don't want to be disturbed. No visitors. I won't talk to anyone!"

"Yes sir, Mr. Tumbleweed," Mr. Plinkus replied.

Tex hurried toward the elevator. A hand-some young man with wavy blond hair rushed up to him. The blond man spoke to Tex in excitement, waving his arms in the air. The elevator doors opened. The blond man and Tex both stepped inside.

"Hmmm. That's strange," I told Ashley. "Tex wanted to be alone. Why did he talk to—"

Eeeeeeeeaaaaaaah!

An earsplitting scream filled the lobby.

Chapter 5

Ashley and I leaped out from behind our potted plant.

Mr. Plinkus rushed out from behind the desk.

Elvis flapped his wings and fluttered into the air.

Eeeeeeeeeaaaaaaaah!

Another horrible shriek rang out. The screams were coming from outside near the pool.

"Oh, dear, what now?" Mr. Plinkus exclaimed. He rushed out to the pool. Ashley and I tore off our disguises and followed him.

"It's Miss Monica!" Mr. Plinkus cried. "Oh, please don't scream, Miss Monica," he told the actress. "Help is here!"

The screaming stopped.

Monica gave Mr. Plinkus a big smile. She was wearing a shiny gold bathing suit and matching high-heeled shoes. Her thick brown hair was pinned up, and she was wearing a hat. It was black and trimmed with curly white feathers. A scarf made of green feathers hung around her neck.

"Thank goodness you came. I'm so upset!" Monica said. "I was lying here soaking up the sun. Then I reached for my silver compact to powder my nose." Tears welled up in her eyes. "But my compact was gone!"

Ashley wrote in her notebook. MISSING: Monica's silver compact.

"I must get that compact back," Monica went on. "It brings me good luck! I'm trying out for a big part in a movie this week. The *main* role. I can't possibly get the part without that compact."

"Can you tell us where you last saw the

compact?" I asked Monica.

She pointed to a small table next to her chair. "I put it right there," she told me.

I studied the table with my magnifying glass. "There's nothing here now—except for your pineapple drink and these sunflower seeds," I said.

Ashley pulled a plastic bag and a pair of tweezers from the pocket of her trenchcoat. She used the tweezers to lift the seeds off the table. She dropped the seeds into the bag and held it up to Monica.

"Were you eating sunflower seeds?" she asked.

"Why, no," Monica said. "I hate sunflower seeds."

"Was Tex Tumbleweed near here, eating sunflower seeds?" Ashley asked.

"I don't know if anyone was nearby," Monica replied. "I had my eyes closed."

Brriiing!

Mr. Plinkus grabbed his cellular phone

from his jacket pocket. He spoke into it briefly. "Not again!" he cried in horror. "Get out of there—fast!"

Mr. Plinkus turned to Ashley and me. "That was Tex Tumbleweed," he whispered. "He's calling from his living room. Someone is in his bedroom!"

Chapter 6

Tex Tumbleweed was pacing the hall outside his room. He had a worried look on his face.

"Shhh!" he warned us, raising a finger to his lips. "Listen. Do you hear that? There's someone groaning in my bedroom!"

Ashley and I pressed our ears to the door so we could listen.

La-la-la-la-laaaaaaaaaaaaaaaaaaaaaaaaa!

"That's not groaning," I told Tex. "That's singing!"

"Singing?" Tex frowned. "Why would someone be in my room singing?" he asked.

"Let's be logical," Ashley told him. "You're making a movie called *The Singing Cowboy Gets Rich*."

"Yes, but I don't see what that has to do

with anything," Tex said.

"*I* see," I told him. "Ashley thinks that someone is in your room singing—because they're trying out for the part of the singing cowboy in your movie."

"That's what I think, all right," Ashley said with a nod.

"Sounds good to me," Mr. Plinkus added.

"But that's *not* logical," Tex replied. "I don't hold tryouts in my hotel room."

"Then there's only one thing to do—go into your bedroom and see who's inside," Ashley said.

Tex opened the door.

The four of us tiptoed into the bedroom.

It was large and bright.

Sunlight streamed in through the sliding glass doors to the balcony.

The balcony doors were open, and a warm breeze blew through the room.

"Why, no one's here!" Tex exclaimed in surprise.

"But they could have run out through these sliding doors," Ashley said.

Ashley stepped onto the balcony. "No one's here now," she called.

We all hurried back to the living room.

"Oh, no!" Tex stared at the table near the living room balcony.

He shook his head in dismay.

"What's wrong?" I asked him.

Tex's face turned red.

"My bolo tie! I took it off before I ran out. Now it's missing!"

"Do you mean that string tie with the shiny silver star clasp?" Ashley asked.

"That's the one," Tex told her.

"Is it worth a lot of money?" I asked.

"No, but that tie is very special to me," Tex replied.

"How come?" Ashley asked.

"I bought it the day I dug my first gushing oil well," Tex answered. "The day I became rich."

"Oh, my, oh, my!" Mr. Plinkus said. His face crumpled, and for a minute he looked as if he might begin to cry.

There was a knock on the door.

Tex flung it open, and a waiter strolled in, pushing a cart.

On the cart rested a silver platter filled with sunflower seeds.

"These seeds are a gift from Lance Lucky," the waiter announced before he left the room.

"Why, that's mighty nice of him!" Tex exclaimed. "I wonder how he knew I love sunflower seeds."

"Who's Lance Lucky?" I asked.

"Oh, he's a young actor fellow," Tex replied. "He wants to play the part of the singing cowboy in my movie."

"Is Lance Lucky the blond man you were talking to in the elevator?" I asked.

"Sure enough, little partner," Tex said. "He's a good actor. But I think he's too quiet to play the part of Tex Tumbleweed."

Tex drew himself up to his full height. "I'm a big man with big emotions," he said. "I laugh, I cry, I shout!"

Just then I heard voices shouting outside the hotel. "Who is making all that noise?" Ashley asked.

Ashley and I rushed to the balcony. The voices were coming from the pool below.

"It's Monica," I said. "And she's arguing with Lance!"

As we watched, Monica leaped forward and gave Lance a shove. His legs flew out from under him.

Splash!

Lance landed in the pool.

"I'd better go help!" Mr. Plinkus rushed to the door.

"We'd better check it out, too," I said.

Ashley and I raced out of Tex's room.

We flew through the door and out into the hall.

Kabooom!

We smacked into something huge—and fell to the floor!

We're Mary-Kate and Ashley—the Trenchcoat
Twins. There we were on vacation in Hawaii,
exploring the island on our bikes.

Our family was staying in a fancy hotel. It had everything a kid could want—a big swimming pool, a video arcade—it even had its very own cockatoo!

We couldn't wait to check out the huge TV in our room. But first we had a mystery to solve.

The hotel manager, Mr. Plinkus, said some guests had been robbed—and he *really* needed our help to catch the thief!

We were on the case. We looked around for suspicious characters.

Then we heard a loud scream from the hotel pool area. It was Monica, the movie star. A thief had stolen her silver make-up case!

**And Tex, the billionaire, was robbed, too. His
special silver-star tie was taken from his room!**

Then Luigi the opera singer's silver pitch pipe disappeared from his dressing room! Luigi was *very* upset! We had to catch this thief—and fast.

Ashley and I went over and over the clues in the case. We realized that the thief only stole from guests on the fifth floor. Hmmmm.

Only one person on the fifth floor had *not* been robbed—a man named Lance. He was our main suspect. So we watched him closely.

Mr. Plinkus let us into Lance's room and—BINGO! On his balcony we found all the missing items! We rushed to the lobby to give everyone the good news.

"Good job, partner!" We congratulated each other for solving another tough case. But wait!

Lance *wasn't* the thief! You'll never believe who the *real* thief was. We figured it out. Can you?

Chapter 7

Ashley and I glanced up. We had bumped into a very plump man with a very large stomach wrapped in a very colorful sash.

"Luigi!" Mr. Plinkus exclaimed. "Pardon us, please!"

"You are pardoned!" Luigi said. He had a booming voice with a strong Italian accent. He bent over Ashley and me. "Are you small ladies hurt?" he asked.

We shook our heads no. Luigi stretched out a hand and helped us stand up.

"Wait—you dropped your whistle," Ashley said. She picked up a shiny, round silver object from the floor and handed it to Luigi. He clutched it and beamed at Ashley.

"Thank you! But this is no whistle," Luigi

told her. "This is my pitch pipe. I blow into it to hear the musical notes. Then I know which notes to sing. I can't sing at all without it!"

"I'm glad you didn't lose it, then," Ashley said.

"Yes, to lose this would be so very sad," Luigi told us. "Much worse than losing the diamond belt buckle that was stolen from my room."

Luigi glared at Mr. Plinkus.

Mr. Plinkus turned bright red.

"This pipe was made in Italy," Luigi went on. "There is no other pitch pipe so fine in all the world." He blew into the pipe. "La-la-la-la-la-laaaaaa," he sang.

Ashley and I exchanged looks of surprise. It was the same singing we just heard in Tex Tumbleweed's room!

"Could Luigi have been singing in Tex's room?" Ashley whispered to me.

"I don't think so," I replied. "That person

had to sneak away across the balcony. And Luigi is awfully heavy to be climbing over balconies."

"That's true," Ashley said. "But Great-grandma Olive would tell us to keep an open mind. So I guess it's possible."

"Right." I turned to Luigi. "Excuse me," I said. "But where were you about five minutes ago?"

"Why, I was in my room," Luigi replied. "I was working up my courage for my big moment."

"What big moment?" I asked.

"The big moment when I talk to Mr. Tumbleweed," Luigi said.

Tex stepped into the hall. Luigi's dark eyes lit up. "Mr. Tumbleweed! I am Luigi Caprio, the great opera star."

"Howdy-do," Tex said, shaking Luigi's hand.

"I must speak to you about something most important," Luigi said. "But it is private.

51

May we talk in your room?"

"I suppose I can give you five minutes," Tex agreed. He threw an arm around Luigi's shoulders. They stepped into his room together. Tex closed the door behind them.

"Ashley—we forgot!" I cried. "We have to find out why Monica pushed Lance into the pool. Come on!"

Ashley, Mr. Plinkus, and I hurried down to the pool. But when we arrived, Monica and Lance were already gone. Mr. Plinkus sighed. "I hope they're all right now," he said.

"We can talk to them later," I replied.

Ashley and I headed across the lobby just as Trent pushed his way through the revolving doors. We giggled. Seaweed was tangled in Trent's hair. His surfing shorts were twisted around his legs. He was covered with sand.

"How was surfing?" I asked.

"Wipeout city," Trent replied with a scowl. "I fell off my surfboard about a million times!

Surfing is a lot harder than it looks."

"Where are Mom and Dad and Lizzie?" Ashley asked.

"Right behind me," Trent said.

Our parents strolled through the revolving door. Lizzie came after them, holding Clue's leash.

"I hope that cute Elvis is still here," Lizzie said.

"Elvis is at the front desk," I told her.

"Grrrrr...woof!" Clue dragged Lizzie toward the desk, pulling at her leash.

"Clue, stop, girl!" Lizzie cried. "Down!"

Clue paid no attention.

Mom shook her head. "I don't know what's wrong with Clue," she said. "She behaved better *before* she started going to obedience school!"

Dad nodded sadly. "I guess it was a waste of money," he said. "Clue will never pass her obedience school test."

Elvis saw Clue coming and leaped off his

perch. He flapped his wings. He flew through the open doors to the pool and disappeared.

"Oh, no," Lizzie said. "Elvis flew away!"

"Don't worry about Elvis," Mr. Plinkus told her. "His wings have been clipped."

"That must have hurt! Poor Elvis," Lizzie said.

"No, no. It didn't hurt him at all," Mr. Plinkus said. "Clipping his wings just keeps Elvis from flying too far."

"I guess you'll have to talk to Elvis another time," I told Lizzie.

"Forget about that bird," Trent said. He rubbed his arm. "My elbow is sore," he said. "I banged it when I fell off my surfboard. I want to go upstairs."

"Good idea," Mom told him. "We'll put some ice on your arm to make it feel better." Mom pushed the button for the elevator.

I grabbed Clue's leash. "Come on, girl," I said. "You're coming with us for a while."

"Where are you and Ashley going?" Dad asked.

"You'd better go to room 506," Mr. Plinkus answered. He had just hung up the hotel phone, and his hands trembled.

"What's in room 506?" Ashley asked.

"Another robbery!" Mr. Plinkus exclaimed.

Chapter 8

"Luigi is in room 506. And his pitch pipe was stolen!" Mr. Plinkus told us as we raced down the fifth-floor hall.

We found Luigi in his living room. He paced back and forth in front of the balcony doors.

"Tell us everything," I said.

"They did it!" Luigi shouted. "They want to keep me from singing! *All* of them!"

"All of *who*?" I asked.

Luigi's plump cheeks turned red. "The ones who want to play the singing cowboy. That's who!" Luigi swung his arms up in the air. "They want the role, but they can't even sing! What good is a singing cowboy who can't sing? I'll tell you—no good! Only the great Luigi can bring music to the role." Luigi paused and wiped sweat off his forehead.

"Wait a minute," I said. "*You* want to play the singing cowboy?"

"And why not?" Luigi asked.

Ashley and I stared at Luigi. He was short and plump and round. Tex Tumbleweed was tall and slim.

"Uh, you don't look much like Tex," I said, trying to be polite. "And you don't sound like you come from Texas."

"I can learn to talk like a Texan," Luigi said.

"But you don't sing cowboy songs," Ashley added. "You sing opera."

Luigi glared. "But *they* cannot sing at *all*!" he shouted. "Not Lance or Monica. *Her* only talent is to scream!"

"Monica?" I asked in confusion. "How could she play the part of Tex Tumbleweed?"

"Monica wants Tex to change his movie. She wants him to change it to *The Singing*

Cowgirl *Gets Rich*," Luigi explained.

"So that's the big role she's trying out for," Ashley said.

"Grrrrr…woof!"

Clue raced to the balcony and started barking again.

"Not now, Clue," I said. "Stop misbehaving!"

"Wait!" Ashley told me. "Maybe Clue is barking at this!" She stooped down near the balcony doors. She pulled a curly white feather out from under the table.

"Is this your feather?" Ashley asked Luigi.

"I have never seen that feather before," Luigi said.

"But I have," I said. "It looks exactly like the curly white feathers on Monica's black hat."

"I knew it! Monica is the thief!" Luigi shouted. "She must have dropped the feather when she took my pitch pipe!"

"The case is solved. Thank goodness!" Mr.

Plinkus exclaimed.

"Wait! We have no proof that Monica is the thief," I said. "This feather is just another clue."

Ashley pulled out her notebook and flipped to our list of clues. "We have sunflower seeds, the sound of singing in Tex's room, and now this curly white feather," she said.

Hmmmmm.

"Monica's compact was stolen outside. But everything else was stolen from a table near a balcony," I added. "That's a lot of information. But none of it adds up to anything."

"Don't worry," Ashley told Mr. Plinkus. "We'll figure out this case, and soon. We always solve the crime by dinner time."

Mr. Plinkus checked his watch. "I eat dinner at five o'clock," he said. "And it's after four thirty. You have less than thirty minutes to catch the thief."

Thirty minutes? *Gulp!*

"No problem," I said. "We'll just do what we always do when we're stumped."

"What do we always do?" Ashley whispered to me.

"Uh—we go over our clues one more time," I replied. I grabbed Clue's leash. I waved good-bye to Luigi and Mr. Plinkus.

"Where to?" Ashley asked as we hurried down the hall.

"Back to our room," I said.

We hurried into our room. Ashley and I took out our laptop computers. We typed in all the clues from our notebook.

"Okay," I said. "Now let's review the facts. We know that Monica and Lance want to play Tex in the movie, but they can't sing. Luigi *can* sing, and he wants the role, but he can't climb balconies."

Ashley frowned. "I'm still stumped," she said. "Let's start over. Let's not ask *who* stole the missing items. Let's ask *what* was stolen."

Ashley typed into her computer: LIST OF

60

"First there were Monica's necklace and Luigi's diamond-studded belt buckle," Ashley said as she typed. "They were stolen before we arrived at the hotel."

"And then Mom's gold charm bracelet was taken," I added. "Then Monica's compact, and then Tex's silver bolo tie."

"And now Luigi's silver pitch pipe." Ashley finished the list. "Okay," she said. "How are all those things alike?"

"Well, all of the things are small," I said. "That makes them easy for the thief to slip into his pocket."

"Yes. And don't forget that all of them are shiny," Ashley added.

"Right. And that means…" I shook my head in confusion. "I don't know what it means," I said.

Ashley and I exchanged worried looks. Our questions weren't helping. They were making things worse!

I glanced at my watch. "It's way after four thirty now," I said. "We're almost out of time."

Ashley's eyes lit up. "That gives me an idea for another question! What *time* were the things stolen?" she asked.

"They were all stolen in the daytime," I said.

"Yes! And it's easier to see then," Ashley said. "So…"

"So…?" I asked.

"So…nothing," Ashley answered. "We're still stumped! I have no idea who the thief is. Do you?"

"No," I said. "But I *do* have a hunch."

"Hooray!" Ashley cried. "What's your hunch, Mary-Kate?" she asked.

I tried to smile. "I have a hunch that this is one crime that Olsen and Olsen *won't* solve by dinner time!"

Chapter 9

"I hate to say this, Mary-Kate, but I think you're right. We'd better give up," Ashley said. "I'm out of questions—and ideas."

I sighed. "Let's take Clue for a walk. We can think some more and review the facts again," I said.

We led Clue down the four flights of stairs to the lobby. It looked quiet and calm. Elvis was still away, flying around somewhere. Mr. Plinkus was bent over his desk, quietly working.

"I guess we should tell Mr. Plinkus that we *can't* solve this mystery," I said.

Ashley nodded. We walked slowly up to Mr. Plinkus.

"Ah, Mary-Kate! Ashley!" he said. "It's almost five o'clock! Did you catch the thief yet?"

"Well, you see," I began. "It's just that this case is a little bit more confusing than any of our other cases."

"There are so many suspects," Ashley went on. "So many people who want a part in this movie. Monica, Luigi, Lance. And they were all robbed, and they all—"

"Oh, Lance wasn't robbed," Mr. Plinkus said.

Ashley and I exchanged looks of surprise.

I smacked my hand against my forehead. "You're right! Lance *wasn't* robbed!"

Ashley flipped through our notebook. "We know that Lance bought a lot of sunflower seeds for Tex," she read.

"Maybe Lance is the thief!" I exclaimed. "He could be stealing things to raise money to buy Tex gifts!"

I counted on my fingers. "Lance is the

only one who wasn't robbed. And he's the only one who isn't a guest in the hotel."

"Oh, but Lance *is* a guest!" Mr. Plinkus exclaimed. "He's in room 504. I was just writing out the paperwork now. Lance *was* a guest on the tenth floor, but he moved to the fifth floor last night. I didn't know about it because I wasn't working last night." Mr. Plinkus sighed. "I imagine he moved to be closer to Tex Tumbleweed."

"Or to make it easier for him to steal Tex's bolo tie," I said. "This information could make Lance our number-one suspect."

"But none of this is proof," Ashley reminded me.

"I think I know where to find some proof. In room 504," I said.

"This is a serious situation," Mr. Plinkus said. "So I give you permission to enter Lance's room. I'll even unlock the door for you."

"Fantastic!" I said. "Room 504, here we

come!" I grabbed Clue's leash.

Mr. Plinkus let us into Lance's room. He went back down to the lobby.

"Look at this, Mary-Kate." Ashley hurried up to the coffee table in the living room. She lifted an article that had been clipped from a newspaper. The clipping told all about Tex Tumbleweed's movie. Under the clipping was a cassette tape.

"This is a tape of Luigi's greatest opera hits," she said. She flipped the tape over. "The photo on the back shows Luigi with his silver pitch pipe. It says right here that he can't sing without it."

Next to the tape were three bags of sunflower seeds. Lying under the bags was a movie magazine. On the cover of the magazine was a big, colorful photograph of Monica.

A curly white feather was stuck in the pages of the magazine as a bookmark. I opened the magazine. "This article tells how

Monica can't try out for a movie role without her good-luck compact," I said.

"It looks like Lance was collecting information about what to steal from Luigi and Monica," Ashley said.

"Yes, but that's still not proof that he's the thief," Ashley told me.

"Grrrrr...woof!"

Clue ran past us and leaped up at the curtains that covered the balcony doors.

"Here we go again," I muttered. "Down, Clue! Be careful, girl," I scolded. "You'll rip these curtains!"

I pushed the curtains aside. Something bright and shiny gleamed on the balcony.

"Ashley!" I exclaimed. "Come here, quick! You'll never believe what Clue just found!"

Chapter 10

I slid open the balcony doors and rushed outside.

"What is it?" Ashley asked.

"Proof!" I said. I bent and lifted a small basket. Inside the basket was everything that had been stolen—Monica's necklace and compact, Luigi's belt buckle and pitch pipe, Tex's bolo tie, and Mom's bracelet.

"We'd better call Mr. Plinkus," Ashley said.

I rushed back into the room and phoned Mr. Plinkus at the front desk. "We know who the thief is!" I told him. "Call everyone and have them meet us at the front desk."

"Will do," Mr. Plinkus said.

I stooped down and gave Clue a giant hug. "Good girl," I told her. "You found everything that was stolen!"

I grabbed the basket with the stolen items. Ashley scooped up the movie magazine with the feather bookmark, the tape of Luigi, and the clipping about Tex Tumbleweed. We brought everything down to the lobby.

Monica, Tex, Luigi, and Lance were already waiting near the front desk. Mr. Plinkus joined the group.

"What's going on, little partners?" Tex asked.

"We solved the case," I said.

"We know who the thief is," Ashley added.

"Great! Who is it?" Lance asked.

Ashley and I stared at him in surprise. "Why, it's you!" I told him.

"Me?" Lance's mouth dropped open in surprise.

"Yes. And here's the proof," I said. I held up the basket. "All the stolen items were in this basket on your balcony."

"Do not pretend you didn't do it," Luigi told him. "They caught you red-handed!"

"Your chances of being the singing cowboy are over," Monica added. She smiled.

Lance's mouth dropped open. His eyebrows shot up. "That's crazy! You're all wrong!" he exclaimed. "I never stole anything in my life!"

"Then how do you explain this?" Ashley asked. She held up the movie magazine with the feather bookmark, the tape of Luigi, and the clipping about Tex Tumbleweed.

"Weren't you doing research to learn which items to steal?" I asked.

"No! Of course not," Lance replied. "I needed to learn more about Tex so I could play him in the movie. And I wanted to know more about Luigi because he also was after the part. Monica is my favorite movie star," he added. "I read about her all the time."

Lance turned to Tex. He dropped onto one knee. His lips trembled, and a tear rolled down his cheek. "Please, Mr. Tumbleweed, you must believe me," Lance begged. "I didn't do it! I'm an innocent man!"

"But if you didn't do it—" I began to say. I stopped as Lizzie raced across the lobby. Mom, Dad, and Trent were right behind her.

"Look, Mary-Kate! Look, Ashley," Lizzie called. "See what I got? A fancy new ring!"

Lizzie held up her hand. In her palm rested a huge, shiny toy ring with a giant fake diamond in the center.

"Uh, that's really pretty, Lizzie," I said. "But we can't talk now. We're trying to solve this case."

Mom and Dad pulled Lizzie aside. Trent rolled his eyes.

Monica pointed at Lance. "I *know* you're the thief!" she told him. "You plucked feathers from my hat. Then you left them in Luigi's room to make *me* look like the thief!"

Lance blinked in dismay. His eyes grew misty. "You're wrong, Monica," he said. "I just wanted something that belonged to you. I wanted to prove that I met you and spoke to you in person."

"Spoke to me?" Monica shrieked. "You tried to talk me into playing the part of the singing cowboy's *girlfriend*!" Monica fumed. "You wanted me to take a small role—so you could have the main role for yourself!"

Lance stood up straighter. "Please! Let's not argue about it again," he said.

"Wait a minute," I told him. "Is that what you were arguing about when Monica pushed you into the pool?" I asked.

"Certainly," Monica replied. She shook her head, and the white feathers in her hat bounced up and down. "Lance is the thief. You have the proof in the basket you found on his balcony!"

"But I never saw that basket before in my life! I'm afraid of heights," Lance said, looking fearful. "I never went out on my balcony. I couldn't even look at it. That's why I moved my room to a lower floor—the tenth floor was too scary for me."

"Wait a minute," Ashley said. "Didn't you move to the fifth floor to be closer to Tex?" she asked.

"No!" Lance replied. "In fact, I really wanted to be on the first floor. But there weren't any empty rooms."

"That's true—there weren't," Mr. Plinkus said.

"I still don't believe it!" Monica said angrily. "You're a big fibber," she told Lance.

"Hold on, there. Don't call this young fellow a fibber," Tex told Monica. "I offered to let Lance try out for the main role in my movie. I asked him to meet me on the sundeck, on the roof of the hotel. Lance refused. He was too scared to go on the roof."

"He was?" Monica asked.

"Yes. I believe that proves he's afraid of

high places," Tex said.

"You see?" Lance shouted with glee. "I'm telling the truth! I could never climb around balconies or steal from anybody!"

"But what about this feather?" Ashley held up the curly feather we found in Luigi's room. "Who took this from Monica's hat and dropped it in Luigi's room?"

"Wait. Let me see that feather," Monica said. I handed it to her, and she studied it. "This feather isn't from my hat," she said, looking confused. "It's not as curly as my hat feathers."

"Then whose feather is it?" I asked.

Something swooped into the lobby.

"Elvis!" Lizzie shouted. "Look at my new ring!" Lizzie held up her hand. Elvis dived at Lizzie and scooped the ring off her palm. He carried it away to his perch.

"Elvis! I said to *look* at my ring, not *take* it," Lizzie scolded.

Uh-oh.

I looked at Ashley. Ashley looked back at me.

"Are you thinking what I'm thinking?" I asked her.

"I think so," Ashley said.

I felt my face turn bright red. I took a deep breath. "It looks like we caught the wrong thief," I told everyone.

"But now we know who the *real* thief is!" Ashley exclaimed.

Chapter 11

"It's Elvis! He's the thief!" Ashley said.

"Of course!" Mom said. "Lots of birds like bright, shiny things. I once had a pet parakeet. He loved to play with shiny bird toys."

"So does Elvis," Ashley said. "He saw these shiny things and flew in the open balcony doors to take them."

"That's why nothing was stolen from me," Lance said. "I never opened my balcony doors!"

"I'm just glad to have my pitch pipe back," Luigi said. He lifted it from the basket and blew into it. "La-la-la-laaaaaa!" he sang.

"La-la-la-laaaaaa!" Elvis sang. He sounded exactly like Luigi.

"We heard Elvis singing in Tex's room," I

explained. "And it was his white feather that we found under Luigi's table."

"What about the sunflower seeds?" Monica asked.

"Tex fed sunflower seeds to Elvis. He dropped some when he grabbed your compact," Ashley replied.

"Then the case really is solved?" Mr. Plinkus asked.

"Case closed—by dinner time," I told him. I turned to Lance. "We're sorry we called you a thief," I said.

"That's okay," Lance replied. "I feel better now that everyone knows the truth."

"We don't usually make such big mistakes," Ashley added. "We forgot the most important rules of being good detectives. We forgot to pay attention to *every* detail."

"And we forgot to keep an open mind," I added. "We thought the thief was someone who was trying to get a part in Tex's movie. We decided the answer to the mystery *before* we solved the case," I said. "We'll never make *that* mistake again!"

Mr. Plinkus shook his head. "But there's something I still don't understand," he told us. "Elvis can't fly up to the fifth-floor balconies. His wings were clipped months ago!"

"Do clipped wings grow back?" Ashley asked Mr. Plinkus.

Mr. Plinkus turned red. "Well, yes." He groaned. "I was supposed to have them clipped again, but I never did."

"And Elvis's wings grew back enough to let him fly up to the fifth floor," I said.

Tex Tumbleweed chuckled. "That big chicken was the thief all along—and nobody knew!" he exclaimed.

"Actually one of us did know. Clue!" I said. "She smelled Elvis's scent on the balconies. We thought she was being disobedient. But she was really trying to tell us that Elvis was the thief!"

Mom and Dad knelt down and patted

Clue's head. "Sorry, girl," Mom said.

"We should have known you weren't really misbehaving," Dad added.

"I'm sorry too," Mr. Plinkus said. "Elvis didn't mean any harm."

Tex Tumbleweed waved his big hand. "No harm done. Besides, this all helped me decide who should play the singing cowboy."

"It did?" I asked.

"Yes. Lance will be my singing cowboy," Tex said. He turned to Lance. "I thought you didn't have big emotions. But in the last five minutes, you laughed, you cried, you were sad and angry and strong. Young fellow, you will be a great actor!"

Lance shook Tex's hand. "Thank you, sir! I'll be the best singing cowboy you ever heard!"

"That's not all," Tex went on. "Monica, I'll write a special part just for you. I see that you can do a lot more than scream. And,

Luigi, you will play my beloved father. Nobody knows this, but my father was an opera singer. He taught me to sing. That's how I became the singing cowboy in the first place!"

Monica and Luigi cheered.

Tex turned to Ashley and me. "How would you gals like a job in my movie, too?" he asked.

"No, thanks," I told him. "As soon as this vacation is over, we're going back to our detective agency. And Clue has to get home. She has a test to pass—at obedience school." I patted Clue's head. "Good girl," I said.

"Good girl," Elvis repeated. Clue leaped up and started barking at Elvis.

"Oh, no," Lizzie said. "Clue is misbehaving *again*!"

"No, I think Clue wants to ask a question," I said. "She wants to know how we'll keep Elvis from stealing anymore."

"I absolutely refuse to lock him in a cage,"

Mr. Plinkus said to all of us.

"You won't have to," I told him. "Just teach Elvis *not* to steal."

"How will I ever do that?" Mr. Plinkus asked.

"Easy." I grinned. "Send him to obedience school—for cockatoos!"

Hi — from both of us!

Aloha, Hawaii! It was time to leave this fantastic island. Another case was closed!

Now we were off to sunny Mexico where all sorts of weird things were happening. The earth was shaking. We found snow in the hot jungle. But worst of all, we were being chased by a mysterious silver monster! What did it all add up to? One incredible mystery!

Could we crack the case? Read all about it in *The Case Of The Volcano Mystery*. In the meantime, if you have any questions, you can write us at:

MARY-KATE + ASHLEY'S FUN CLUB
859 HOLLYWOOD WAY, SUITE 412
BURBANK, CA 91505
We would love to hear from you!

Love
Mary-Kate and Ashley

The Adventures of MARY-KATE & ASHLEY™

Look for the best-selling detective home video episodes.

You're Invited to MARY-KATE & ASHLEY'S™

Join the fun!

And also available:

DUALSTAR VIDEO

The Adventures of Mary-Kate & Ashley™ Hawaiian Sweepstakes

OFFICIAL RULES:

1. No purchase necessary.

2. To enter complete the official entry form at participating retailer or hand-print your name, address, and phone number along with the words "The Adventures of Mary-Kate & Ashley™ Hawaiian Sweepstakes" on a 3 x 5 card and mail to: The Adventures of Mary-Kate & Ashley™ Hawaiian Sweepstakes, c/o Scholastic Trade Marketing Dept., P.O. Box 7500, Jefferson City, MO 65102-7500, postmarked no later than August 29,1997. Enter as often as you wish, but each entry must be mailed separately. One entry per envelope. Partially completed, illegible or mechanically reproduced entries will not be accepted. Sponsors and "Hilton" not responsible for lost, late, mutilated, illegible, stolen, postage due, incomplete or misdirected entries. All entries become the property of Scholastic Inc. and will not be returned.

3. Sweepstakes open to all legal residents of the United States who are between the ages of five and twelve by August 29, 1997, excluding employees and immediate family members of Scholastic Inc., Parachute Press, Inc., Warner Vision Entertainment, Dualstar Entertainment Group, Inc., Hilton, and their respective parent companies, affiliates, subsidiaries, advertising, promotion and fulfillment agencies, and the persons with whom each of the above are domiciled. Offer void where prohibited, taxed or restricted.

4. Odds of winning depend on total number of entries received. All prizes will be awarded. Winners will be randomly drawn on or about September 8, 1997, by Scholastic Inc., whose decisions are final. Potential winners will be notified by mail and potential winners and traveling companion will be required to sign and return an affidavit of eligibility, a publicity release where lawful and a liability release, all notarized, within 20 days of notification. Prizes won by minors will be awarded to parent or legal guardian, who must sign and return all required legal documents. By acceptance of their prize, winners and traveling companion consent to the use of their names, photographs, likeness, and personal information by Scholastic Inc., Parachute Press, Inc., Dualstar Entertainment Group, Inc., and "Hilton" for publicity purposes without further compensation except where prohibited.

5. One (1) Grand Prize Winner will receive a trip for four to Hawaii. Trip consists of round-trip coach air transportation for four people from the major airport closest to the winner's home to Honolulu, Hawaii, and four consecutive nights at Hilton Hawaiian Village, quad occupancy in one standard room. Accommodations are room and tax only. Winner and traveling companions are responsible for all incidentals and all other charges, except the hotel tax, including but without limitation to meals, gratuities, all taxes and transfers. Winner must be available to travel any five days and four nights between November 21, 1997, and November 30, 1997, or as otherwise rescheduled for an alternative four nights and five days. Travel must include Saturday night stay. Certain blackout dates and other restriction apply. Reservations must be made at least 10 days in advance of destination date. (Total approximate retail value: $4,000.00)

6. Only one prize will be awarded per individual, family, or household. Prizes are non-transferable and cannot be sold or redeemed for cash. No substitutions allowed. No cash substitute available. Any federal, state or local taxes are the responsibility of the winner.

7. By participating in this promotion all participants and prize winners agree that Hilton Hotels Corporation, its partnerships, subsidiaries and affiliates and each of such entities' respective officers, directors, agents and employees (collectively, "Hilton") are not responsible or liable for any injury, loss, illness, litigation or damage that may occur from participation in the promotion or acceptance, possession, use or misuse of prizes. In the event that any dispute arises regarding the meaning or interpretation of these official rules, participants agree that the dispute shall be resolved by applying the laws of New York and that it shall be resolved by and within the courts of the state of New York. The Hilton logo and logotype are registered trademarks of Hilton Hotels Corporation.

8. Additional terms: By participating, entrants agree a) to the official rules and decisions of the judges which will be final in all respects; and b) to release, discharge and hold harmless Scholastic Inc., Parachute Press, Inc., "Hilton," their affiliates, subsidiaries and advertising and promotion agencies from and against any and all liability or damages associated with acceptance, use or misuse of any prize received in this sweepstakes.

9. To obtain the name of the winner, please send your request and a self-addressed stamped envelope (excluding residents of Vermont and Washington) after September 8, 1997, to The Adventures of Mary-Kate & Ashley, Hawaiian Sweepstakes Winners List, c/o Scholastic Trade Marketing Dept., P.O. Box 7500, Jefferson City, MO 65102-7500.

High-Falootin' Fun for the Whole Family!

OWN IT ON VIDEO!

It doesn't matter if you live around the corner…
or around the world…
If you are a fan of Mary-Kate and Ashley Olsen,
you should be a member of

MARY-KATE + ASHLEY'S FUN CLUB™

Here's what you get:
Our Funzine™
An autographed color photo
Two black & white individual photos
A full size color poster
An official **Fun Club**™ membership card
A **Fun Club**™ school folder
Two special **Fun Club**™ surprises
A holiday card
Fun Club™ collectibles catalog
Plus a **Fun Club**™ box to keep everything in

To join Mary-Kate + Ashley's Fun Club™, fill out the form
below and send it along with

U.S. Residents – $17.00
Canadian Residents – $22 U.S. Funds
International Residents – $27 U.S. Funds

MARY-KATE + ASHLEY'S FUN CLUB™
859 HOLLYWOOD WAY, SUITE 275
BURBANK, CA 91505

NAME:_____

ADDRESS:_____

CITY:_____STATE:_____ZIP:_____

PHONE: (____) _____BIRTHDATE:_____